FROSTY the SNOWMAN ™

By Jack Rollins and Steve Nelson

ideals children's books.
Nashville, Tennessee

ISBN-13: 978-0-8249-5656-1
Published by Ideals Children's Books
An imprint of Ideals Publications
A Guideposts Company
Nashville, Tennessee
www.idealsbooks.com

Designed by Georgina Chidlow-Rucker

Printed and bound in China

Leo_ Aug13_2

Frosty the snowman
was a jolly, happy soul,

with a corncob pipe and a button nose
and two eyes made out of coal.

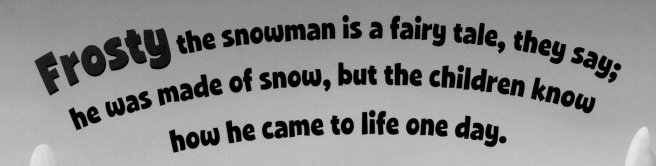

Frosty the snowman is a fairy tale, they say; he was made of snow, but the children know how he came to life one day.

There must have been some magic
in that old silk hat they found,

for when they placed it on his head,
**he began
to dance
around!**

Oh, **Frosty** the snowman
was alive as he could be,
and the children say he could laugh
and play, just the same as you and me.

Frosty the snowman
knew the sun was hot that day,
so he said, "Let's run and we'll have
some fun now, before I melt away."

Down to the village,
with a broomstick in his hand,
running here and there,
all around the square, saying,
"Catch me if you can."

He led them down the streets of town,
right to the traffic cop.
And he only paused a moment
when he heard him holler, "Stop!"

For **Frosty** the snowman
had to hurry on his way,
but he waved goodbye, saying,
"Don't you cry,
I'll be back again someday."

Thumpety-thump-thump,
thumpety-thump-thump,
look at Frosty go,

thumpety-thump-thump,
thumpety-thump-thump,
over the hills of snow.